ASTERIX AND THE SOOTHSAYER

TEXT BY GOSCINNY

DRAWINGS BY UDERZO

TRANSLATED BY ANTHEA BELL AND DEREK HOCKRIDGE

HODDER DARGAUD
LONDON SYDNEY AUCKLAND

ASTERIX IN OTHER COUNTRIES

Australia	Hodder Dargaud, 2 Apollo Place, Lane Cove, New South Wales 2066
Austria	Delta Verlag, Postfach 1215, 7 Stuttgart 1, G.F.R.
Belgium	Dargaud Bénélux, 3 rue Kindermans, 1050 Brussels
Brazil	Cedibra, rua Filomena Nunes 162, Rio de Janeiro
Canada	Dargaud Canada, 307 Benjamin-Hudon, St. Laurent, Montreal P.Q. H4N1J1
Denmark	Gutenberghus Bladene, Vognmagergade 11, 1148 Copenhagen K
Finland	Sanoma Osakeyhtio, Ludviginkatu 2–10, 00130 Helsinki 13
France	Regional Editions
	(Langue d'Oc) Société Toulousaine du Livre, Avenue de Larrieu, 31094 Toulouse
German Federal Republic	Delta Verlag, Postfach 1215, 7 Stuttgart 1, G.F.R.
Greece	Anglo-Hellenic Agency, Kriezotou 3, Syntagma, Athens 134, Greece
Holland	Dargaud Bénélux, 3 rue Kindermans, 1050 Brussels, Belgium
	(Distribution) Oberon, Ceylonpoort 5–25, Haarlem, Holland
Hong Kong	Hodder Dargaud, c/o United Publishers Service Private Ltd, Stanhope House, 734 King's Road
Iceland	Fjolvi HF, Njorvasund 15a, Reykjavik
Indonesia	Pt Sinar Kasih, Tromolpos 260, Jakarta
Israel	Dahlia Pelled Publishers, P.O. Box 33325, Tel Aviv
Italy	Arnoldo Mondadori Editore, 1 Via Belvedere, 37131 Verona
Latin America	Grijalbo-Dargaud S.A., Deu y Mata 98–102, Barcelona 29
New Zealand	Hodder Dargaud, P.O. Box 3858, Auckland 1
Norway	A/S Hjemmet (Gutenburghus Group), Kristian den 4des Gate 13, Oslo 1
Portugal	Meriberica, rua D. Filipa de Vilherna 4–5°, Lisbon 1
Roman Empire	*(Latin)* Delta Verlag, Postfach 1215, 7 Stuttgart 1, G.F.R.
South Africa	*(English)* Hodder Dargaud, P.O. Box 32213, Braamfontein Centre, Braamfontein 2017 Johannesburg
Spain	Grijalbo-Dargaud S.A., Deu y Mata 98–102, Barcelona 29
Sweden	Hemmets Journal Forlag (Gutenburghes Group), Fack, 200 22 Malmo
Switzerland	Interpress Dargaud, En Budron B, 1052 Le Mont/Lausanne
Turkey	Kervan Kitabcilik, Serefendi Sokagi 31, Cagaloglu-Istanbul
Wales	*(Welsh)* Gwasg Y Dref Wen, 28 Church Road, Yr Eglwys Newydd, Cardiff CF4 2EA
Yugoslavia	Nip Forum, Vojvode Misica 1–3, 2100 Novi Sad

— Asterix and the Soothsayer —

ISBN 0 340 19525 8 (cased edition)
ISBN 0 340 20697 7 (paperbound edition)

Copyright © 1972 Dargaud Editeur
English language text copyright © 1975 Hodder & Stoughton Ltd

First published in Great Britain 1975 (cased)
Fourth impression 1979

First published in Great Britain 1976 (paperbound)
Fourth impression 1981

Printed in Great Britain for Hodder Dargaud Ltd,
Mill Road, Dunton Green, Sevenoaks, Kent
by Morrison & Gibb Ltd, London and Edinburgh

The year is 50 BC. Gaul is entirely occupied by the Romans. Well, not entirely... One small village of indomitable Gauls still holds out against the invaders. And life is not easy for the Roman legionaries who garrison the fortified camps of Totorum, Aquarium, Laudanum and Compendium...

a few of the Gauls

Asterix, the hero of these adventures. A shrewd, cunning little warrior; all perilous missions are immediately entrusted to him. Asterix gets his superhuman strength from the magic potion brewed by the druid Getafix...

Obelix, Asterix's inseparable friend. A menhir delivery-man by trade; addicted to wild boar. Obelix is always ready to drop everything and go off on a new adventure with Asterix — so long as there's wild boar to eat, and plenty of fighting.

Getafix, the venerable village druid. Gathers mistletoe and brews magic potions. His speciality is the potion which gives the drinker superhuman strength. But Getafix also has other recipes up his sleeve...

Cacofonix, the bard. Opinion is divided as to his musical gifts. Cacofonix thinks he's a genius. Everyone else thinks he's unspeakable. But so long as he doesn't speak, let alone sing, everybody likes him...

Finally, Vitalstatistix, the chief of the tribe. Majestic, brave and hot-tempered, the old warrior is respected by his men and feared by his enemies. Vitalstatistix himself has only one fear; he is afraid the sky may fall on his head tomorrow. But as he always says, 'Tomorrow never comes.'

5

ASTERIX'S SCEPTICISM HAS NO EFFECT. SUBJECTED TO THE INFLUENCE OF SO MANY GODS, WHO BOTH PROTECT AND THREATEN THEM, THE NATIONS OF ANTIQUITY WOULD LIKE TO HAVE ADVANCE NOTICE OF THEIR WHIMS. HERE WE MUST INSERT A PARENTHESIS...

A PARENTHESIS WHICH IS NECESSARY FOR A BRIEF EXPLANATION OF SOOTHSAYERS ORACLES, PROPHETS, AUGURERS, HARUSPICES AND OTHER INTERPRETERS OF THE SIBYLLINE BOOKS...

O SOOTHSAYER, WILL THE GODS LOOK KINDLY ON THE HARVEST?

SOOTHSAYERS READ THE FUTURE IN THE WAY BIRDS FLY...

YES, FARMER, THE GODS WILL SEND RAIN FOR YOUR FIELDS!

... IN THE APPETITE OF THE SACRED GEESE...

THE GOOSE LIVER PÂTÉ WILL BE GOOD THIS YEAR! THE GODS HAVE SPOKEN!

... AND ABOVE ALL IN THE ENTRAILS OF SACRIFICAL ANIMALS.

YOU CAN SET SAIL. THE GODS WILL BE KIND. THERE'S NOT THE LEAST LITTLE STORM IN THE OFFING.

THE PREDICTIONS OF THE ENTRAILS ARE NOT ALWAYS CORRECT...

I THOUGHT IT WAS JUST A LOAD OF TRIPE!

EVEN THE GREATEST CONSULT THE AUGURIES...

... AND AS LONG AS BRUTUS IS NEAR YOU, O CAESAR, YOU WILL HAVE NOTHING TO FEAR!

IF CERTAIN VISIONARIES HAVE A REASONABLE IDEA OF WHAT THE FUTURE HOLDS...

... GENERALLY THEY SAY ANY OLD THING!

IN SHORT, THEY ARE CHARLATANS WHO THRIVE ON CREDULITY, FEAR AND HUMAN SUPERSTITION. HERE WE CLOSE THE PARENTHESIS.

12

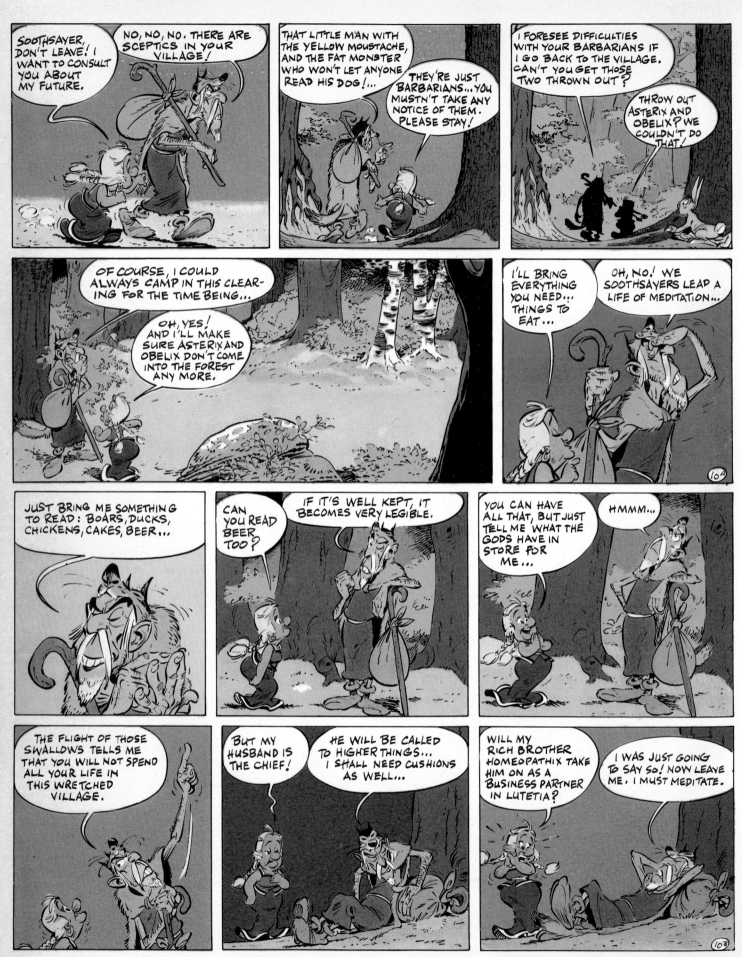

14

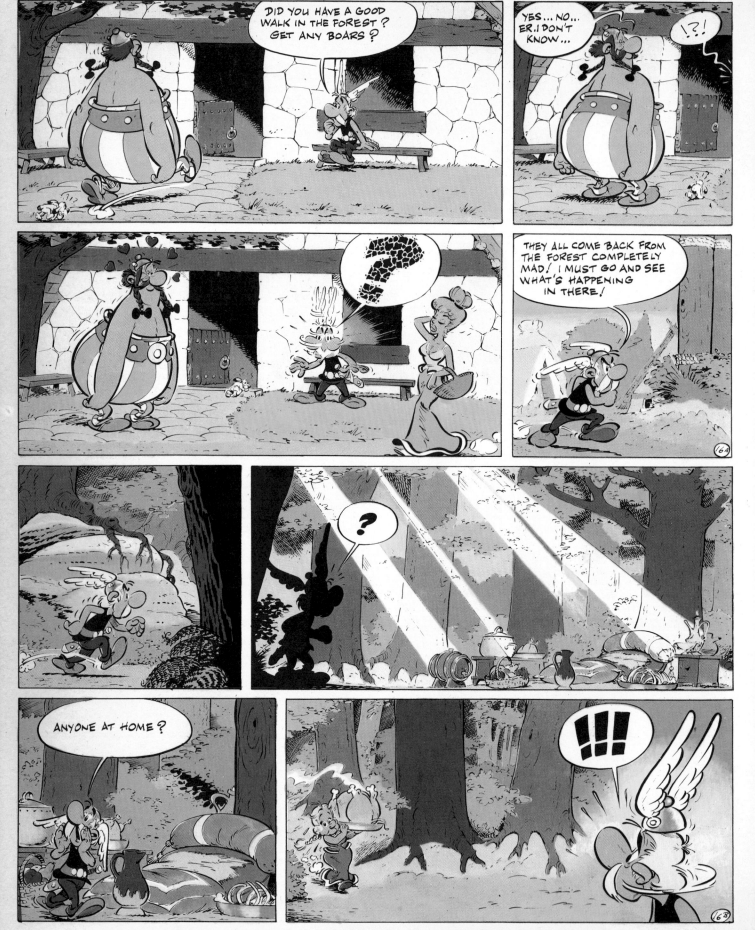

21

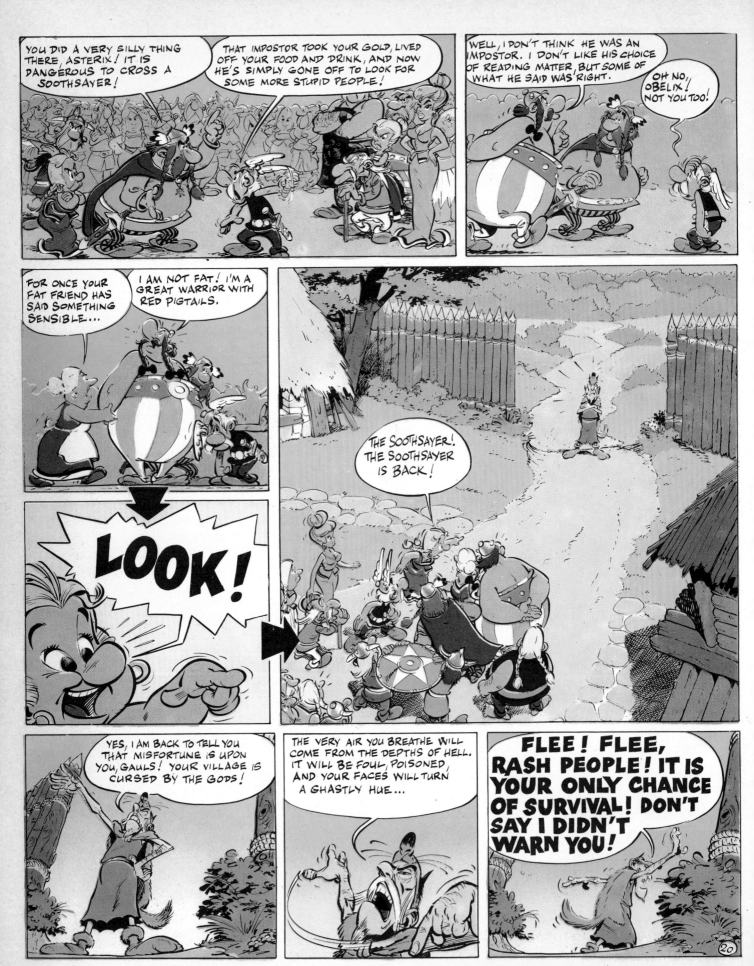

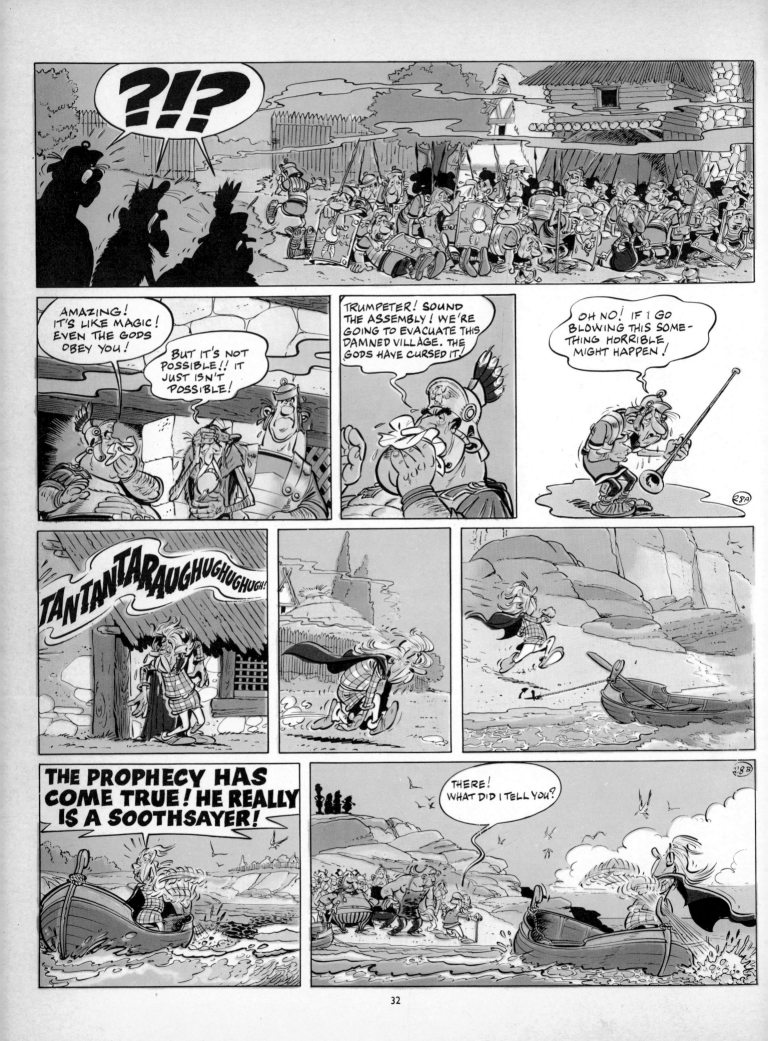

32

33

40

41

43

44